Here's what parents are
Shushybye Baby on BabyFirstTV:

"Right after the bath and teeth, the girls climb on the sofa for *Shushybye Baby!* It's really giving them some very positive associations with the other nightly rituals."

"We are enjoying your amazing show every evening. Shushybye has become part of our bedtime routine. We love all of the songs."

"My son is only 11 months old, but he loves Shushybye. No matter what he's doing, he'll drop it to run to the TV and watch in amazement."

"My granddaughter is in love with the Shushybye crew. She can already sing almost every word to every song! Which is truly amazing to hear, because she just began learning how to talk."

"My daughter LOVES the Shushies!!!"

"We really enjoy all the wonderful music and really cool messages on your new program."

"I just want to let you all know how much my 10-month-old boy loves your show! I am so thankful!"

"My son thinks your show is the best thing in the world (besides his stuffed dog). We watch your show every evening right before his bedtime! How perfect. He loves the music the best!"

Look for the SHUSHYBYE™ television show on BabyFirstTV & Comcast Video on Demand!

Listen to the SHUSHYBYE™ SHOW radio program on XM Satellite Radio's XM Kids!

Learn more about SHUSHYBYE
Visit: www.shushybye.com

Sleepover Surprise

When nighty-night comes
We close our eyes
To dream our dreams
From Shushybye. . . .

Hold the cover of this book under a bright light for a minute and it will glow in the dark!

To our growing legion of honorary Shushies everywhere.
S.S.

For Mom & Dad.
F.C.

For information, address St. Martin's Press, 175 Fifth Avenue, New York, N.Y. 10010.

www.stmartins.com

Printed in China.

Library of Congress Cataloging-in-Publication Data is available
ISBN-13: 978-0-312-37853-0 ISBN-10: 0-312-37853-X

First Edition: April 2008
10 9 8 7 6 5 4 3 2 1

Sleepover Surprise

Written by Stephen Syatt • Illustrated by Frank Caruso

St. Martin's Press • New York

It was a big day
for Leo and Leona.

They were going to stay overnight with Grandma.
The twins sang their favorite Shushybye songs
as Grandma drove them to her house.

Meanwhile, in the Land of Shushybye . . .

the sun was shining, the birds were chirping, and the Candy Cane trees swayed in the gentle breeze. Snoozles was busy making dreams for all the children, while Zeez was doing what Zeez does best—sleeping on the grass.

Just then, along came Dozie, carrying a package of fresh-baked cookies.
"What do you have there, Dozie?" asked Zeez, who woke up as soon as he smelled the delicious aroma.
"It's a little something I baked just for you!" answered Dozie.

Snoozles and Zeez each took a star-shaped cookie from the package.

"These cookies are great!" said Snoozles.
"They sure are! What's the occasion?" asked Zeez.
"You don't need a special occasion to be nice to your friends!" Dozie replied.

Snoozles and Zeez looked at each other. They both had the same idea. They wanted to do something nice for Dozie in return—just because she was such a wonderful friend!

Back at Grandma's house, Leo and Leona were reading their favorite books when Grandma came to tuck them in. "Have you made your Dream Wishes for the night?" asked Grandma.

"I wish to dream about playing Sleepball with Snoozles!" said Leo.
"And I wish to dream about visiting Dozie. She's my favorite Shushy!" said Leona.

Two stars heard their
Dream Wishes and raced
away to give them to the Shushies.
Snoozles and Zeez had just finished making
all their dreams for the night when Snort and
Wheez arrived to take the Dream Boxes to
Conductor McCloud on the Shushybye Train.

"You're just in time to help us think of something nice to do for Dozie!" said Snoozles.
"Is it her birthday?" asked Wheez.
"No," said Zeez, "we just want to do something nice because she is such a cool friend!"

SNORT & WHEEZ
ZZZ

Snort and Wheez placed the last Dream Box into the van when Snort said, "Why don't you take Dozie to see Rockin' Shushy? He's playing at the House of Snooze tonight."

"Rockin' Shushy is Dozie's favorite," said Snoozles. "What a great idea!"

Just then, Zeez spotted two
stars coming down from the sky.

"They're from Leo and Leona!" said Snoozles.

"You'll have to make their dreams quickly!" said Snort. "We're running late to get all these Dream Boxes to Conductor McCloud!"

Snoozles thought for a minute. “Let’s bring Leo and Leona to Shushybye!” he said. “I can play Sleepball with Leo, and then we can all take Dozie to the House of Snooze!”

“Awesome idea, Snoozles!” said Zeez.

With that, Snort and Wheez hurried away in their van.

Snoozles waved his magic Dream Wand, and instantly Snoozles and Zeez were in Leo and Leona's room at Grandma's house.

Leo and Leona were thrilled to see their Shushy friends.

Snoozles and Zeez told them about the surprise for Dozie.

“Can we go, Grandma?” asked Leo.
“It sounds like lots of fun!” said Grandma.

Snoozles waved his Dream Wand again. In a flash, they were all back in Shushybye.
"What a beautiful land this is," said Grandma.

Leo had fun playing Sleepball with Snoozles.

Then they all walked over to Dozie's house.

When Zeez knocked on Dozie's door, she was really surprised. Leona was happy to meet Dozie. And Dozie was delighted to see her friends.

“Guess where you’re going!” cried Snoozles.
“We’re taking you to the House of Snooze
to see Rockin’ Shushy tonight!” said Zeez.
“Wondrous!” Dozie replied.

Dozie and her friends sat at a table right next to the stage. The first performer was everyone's favorite blues singer, Bay B. King.

"I love the blues!" said Zeez. "It's music with feeling!" Then Rockin' Shushy joined Bay B. King onstage to sing "Shushybye Blues."

Leo, Leona, and Grandma clapped along with the Shushies as Rockin' Shushy performed song after song.

After the music, Rockin' Shushy spoke to the audience. "Tonight's show is dedicated to a very special Shushy—someone we love and care about very much—

the one and only, Dozie!"

Everyone stood up and cheered for Dozie as the waiter brought a Sky Pie to the table. It was Dozie's favorite dessert—the perfect ending to such a wonderful surprise.

Leo and Leona were happy that their Dream Wishes had come true, and Grandma was having a great time in Shushybye.

"This is so nice of you!" said Dozie. "But what's the occasion?"

To which all the Shushies replied, "You don't need a special occasion to be nice to your friends!"

Shushybye & Good Night!

Shushybye Blues

Words and Music by Stephen Syatt

When I went to sleep the other night,
You know I kinda put up a fight.
I didn't want to go to sleep so soon.

So my mommy said to me,
You're gonna miss your dreams,
And you'll be singin'—
M-m-m-m-m-m—the Shushybye Blues!

Well, you know, my mommy was right.
I missed my Shushybye Dreams that night.
So from now on, this is what I'm gonna do—

When my mommy says it's time for bed,
I'm gonna lay down my sleepy head.
I won't be singin'—
M-m-m-m-m-m—the Shushybye Blues!

So if you wanna take a tip from me,
Whenever you feel like you're sleepy,
Tell your momma, this is what you're gonna do—
Hop into bed and go nighty-night.
Close your eyes, and sleep real tight.
You won't be singin'—
M-m-m-m-m-m—the Shushybye Blues!